Henry W. Longfellow

Voices of the Night

and other poems

Henry W. Longfellow

Voices of the Night
and other poems

ISBN/EAN: 9783337774332

Printed in Europe, USA, Canada, Australia, Japan

Cover: Foto ©Andreas Hilbeck / pixelio.de

More available books at **www.hansebooks.com**

MAYNARD'S ENGLISH CLASSIC SERIES.—No. 167

VOICES OF THE NIGHT

AND OTHER POEMS

BY

HENRY WADSWORTH LONGFELLOW

With Biographical Sketch, Critical Opinions, and Explanatory Notes

NEW YORK
MAYNARD, MERRILL, & CO.

New Series, No. 113. January 30, 1893. Published Semi-weekly. Subscription Price, $10. Entered at Post Office, New York, as Second-class Matter.

CONTENTS

CRAIGIE HOUSE, LONGFELLOW'S HOME, CAMBRIDGE, MASS.

LIFE OF LONGFELLOW.

THOSE scientists who hold that genius is a morbid distillation from a tainted ancestry would be puzzled to account for Longfellow's undeniable genius. He was descended from two Yorkshire families, whose natural healthiness of mind and body had been developing for several generations in the bracing air of New England. The Longfellows, his father's family, were a sturdy race, who had always done their duty without inquiring into their metaphysical motives for doing it; and his mother's family, the Wadsworths, traced their descent to John Alden,—as wholesome an old Puritan warrior as could well be found.

Henry Wadsworth Longfellow, the poet, was born at Portland, Maine, February 27th, 1807. Like Emerson and Hawthorne, he was a quiet boy, fond of books, and averse to taking part in the sports of his schoolfellows. His

3

nerves shrank from all loud noises. There is a tradition of
his having begged a servant on a glorious Fourth of July
to put cotton in his ears to deaden the roar of the cannon,
and in later life one of his book-plates bore the motto
" Non Clamor, sed Amor."

At the age of fifteen this shy, studious lad was sent to
Bowdoin College at Brunswick, Maine, after Portland
Academy had taught him all it knew. He came prepared
to make the most of his opportunities, and after four years
of hard work graduated with distinction, and with the
promise of a professorship after a year of travel had
broadened his mental horizon.

The next summer found Longfellow at Paris with all
Europe before him. He wandered through England,
France, Germany, Italy, Holland, and Spain ; everywhere
studying the languages, and absorbing the rich associations
of foreign places. His impressions of what he saw were in
later years embodied in the prose works *Outre-Mer* and
Hyperion. On his return he at once assumed the duties of
his professorship, finding little time for literature. In 1831
he married an acquaintance of former years, Mary Storer
Potter, with whom he lived most happily until her prema-
ture death in 1835. In 1834 a pleasant surprise came in the
shape of an offer of the Chair of Modern Languages at
Harvard, an offer which Longfellow was only too glad to
accept. The new professor's official duties were light, and
he had leisure for the literary pursuits which had ever
been his delight. *Hyperion*, a romance in two volumes,
and *The Voices of the Night*, a volume of poems containing
"The Reaper and the Flowers," and "The Psalm of Life,"
were published in 1839. Two years later appeared *Ballads
and other Poems*, containing the " Wreck of the Hesperus,"
"The Village Blacksmith," and " Excelsior "; and in the
following year *Poems on Slavery*. This quiet life of work

was interrupted in 1842 by a visit to Dickens in London, but speedily resumed. In July, 1843, Longfellow married his second wife, a Miss Appleton, whose acquaintance he had made for the first time during his Swiss tour. Longfellow's ambition was to be the national poet of America,—an ambition to which he was spurred on by Margaret Fuller, probably the most intellectual woman of the time in America. She called his poems exotic flowers, with no smell of American soil about them. The outcome of this criticism was the writing of *Evangeline*, followed later by *Hiawatha* and *Miles Standish*, all refreshingly American in flavor. *Hiawatha*, a poem founded on Indian myths, is cast in the form of the Eddas, the ancient epics of Finland, a form with which Longfellow had become familiar in his studies of the Scandinavian languages. *The Courtship of Miles Standish* pictures the deeds and sufferings of the early Plymouth colony, a recital enlivened only by the description of the courting of Priscilla by proxy. It is not to be understood that Longfellow's fame rested on these American poems alone : he had already written a quantity of poetry which had established his reputation as a poet, but it was on these that he based his claim to be considered the national poet of America.

In 1854, after about eighteen years of academic work, Longfellow felt warranted in resigning his Harvard professorship, to be free for purely literary pursuits. His home at Cambridge was the large Craigie House, which could boast of having once been the headquarters of Washington. Here, surrounded by a brilliant circle of friends, he lived in all the flush of a happy, successful life until 1861,—that fatal year,—when his peace was invaded by a frightful calamity: Mrs. Longfellow, while playing with her children, set fire to her dress, and was mortally injured by the flames. The poet never recovered from the shock of this bereavement, although he continued his work with unabated vigor until the time of his death in March 1882.

After Tennyson, Longfellow has been the most popular poet of his day. Some critics have said that had Tennyson never written the *Idylls*, or *In Memoriam*, his inferiority to Longfellow would have been manifest, but the power displayed in these high realms of poetry was quite beyond Longfellow's reach. His range is domestic. He lacks the power of depicting deep passion, or of robing purely imaginative subjects with ideal grace and color. The forces necessary to the execution of an heroic poem are not his, but on the other hand, in such a description of quiet love and devoted patience as he gives us in Evangeline, Longfellow may be ranked with the greatest of poets.

CHRONOLOGICAL LIST OF THE PRINCIPAL WORKS OF LONGFELLOW.

Coplas de Manrique	1833	Tales of a Wayside Inn	1863
Outre-Mer	1835	Flower-De-Luce	1867
Hyperion	1839	Divine Comedy of Dante	
Voices of the Night	1839	Alighieri	1867–70
Ballads and other Poems	1841	New England Tragedies	1868
Poems on Slavery	1842	Divine Tragedy	1871
Spanish Student	1843	Three Books of Song	1872
Poets and Poetry of		Christus	1872
Europe	1845	Aftermath	1873
Belfry of Bruges	1846	Hanging of the Crane	1874
Evangeline	1847	Masque of Pandora	1875
Kavanagh	1849	Kéramos	1878
Seaside and the Fireside	1850	Ultima Thule	1880
Golden Legend	1851	In the Harbor [Ultima	
Hiawatha	1855	Thule, Pt. ii.]	1882
Miles Standish	1858	Michael Angelo	1884

CHILD of New England, and trained by her best influences; of a temperament singularly sweet and serene, and with the sturdy rectitude of his race; refined and softened by wide contact with other lands and many men; born in prosperity, accomplished in all literatures, and himself a literary artist of consummate elegance,—he was the fine flower of the Puritan stock under its changed modern conditions. Out of strength had come forth sweetness. The grim iconoclast, "humming a surly hymn," had issued in the Christian gentleman. Captain Miles Standish had risen into Sir Philip Sidney. The austere morality that relentlessly ruled the elder New England reappeared in the genius of this singer in the most gracious and captivating form. . . . The foundations of our distinctive literature were largely laid in New England, and they rest upon morality. Literary New England had never a trace of literary Bohemia. The most illustrious group, and the earliest, of American authors and scholars and literary men, the Boston and Cambridge group of the last generation,—Channing, the two Danas, Sparks, Everett, Bancroft, Ticknor, Prescott, Norton, Ripley, Palfrey, Emerson, Parker, Hawthorne, Longfellow, Holmes, Whittier, Agassiz, Lowell, Motley,—have been sober and industrious citizens, of whom Judge Sewall would have approved. Their lives as well as their works have ennobled literature. They have illustrated the moral sanity of genius.

Longfellow shares this trait with them all. It is the moral purity of his verse which at once charms the heart; and in his first most famous poem, the "Psalm of Life," it is the direct inculcation of a moral purpose. Those who insist that literary art, like all other art, should not concern itself positively with morality, must reflect that the heart

7

of this age has been touched as truly by Longfellow, however differently, as that of any time by its master-poet. This, indeed, is his peculiar distinction. Among the great poetic names of the century in English literature, Burns, in a general way, is the poet of love; Wordsworth, of lofty contemplation of nature; Byron, of passion; Shelley, of aspiration; Keats, of romance; Scott, of heroic legend; and not less, and quite as distinctively, Longfellow, of the domestic affections. He is the poet of the household, of the fireside, of the universal home feeling. The infinite tenderness and patience, the pathos and the beauty, of daily life, of familiar emotion, and the common scene,—these are the significance of that verse whose beautiful and simple melody, softly murmuring for more than forty years, made the singer the most widely beloved of living men.—*George William Curtis.*

He is in a high sense a literary man; and next a literary artist; and thirdly, a literary artist in the domain of poetry. It would not be true to say that his art is of the intensest kind or most magical potency; but it is art, and imbues whatever he performs. In so far as a literary artist in poetry is a poet, Longfellow is a poet, and should (to the silencing of all debates and demurs) be freely confessed and handsomely installed as such. How far he is a poet in a further sense than this remains to be determined.

Having thus summarily considered "the actual quality of the work" as derived from the endowments of the worker, I next proceed to "the grounds upon which the vast popularity of the poems has rested." One main and in itself all-sufficient ground has just been stated: that the sort of intelligence of which Longfellow is so conspicuous an example includes pre-eminently "a great susceptibility to the spirit of the age." The man who meets the spirit of the age half-way will be met half-way by that; will be adopted as a favorite child, and warmly reposited in the heart. Such has been the case with Longfellow. In sentiment, in percep-

tion, in culture, in selection, in utterance, he represents,
with adequate and even influential but not overwhelm-
ing force, the tendencies and adaptabilities of the time ; he
is a good type of the "bettermost," not the exceptionally
very best, minds of the central or later-central period of the
nineteenth century ; and, having the gift of persuasive
speech and accomplished art, he can enlist the sympathies
of readers who approach his own level of intelligence, and
can dominate a numberless multitude of those who belong
to lower planes, but who share none the less his own general
conceptions and aspirations.

Evangeline, whatever may be its shortcomings and blem-
ishes, takes so powerful a hold of the feelings that the
fate which would at last merge it in oblivion could only be
a very hard and even a perverse one. Who that has read
it has ever forgotten it ? or in whose memory does it rest as
other than a long-drawn sweetness and sadness that has
become a portion, and a purifying portion, of the experi-
ences of the heart ?— *William Michael Rossetti.*

MR. LONGFELLOW was easily first amongst his own coun-
trymen as a poet, and in certain directions as a prose
writer ; but he was also a good deal more than this. There
has been a tendency to doubt whether he was entitled to a
place in the first rank of poets ; and the doubt, although
we are not disposed to think it well founded, is perhaps
intelligible. Some of the qualities which gave his verse
its charm and its very wide popularity and influence also
worked, not to perplex—for the essence of his style was
simplicity—but perhaps to vex, the critical mind. There
is no need to dwell now upon various pieces of verse by
Mr. Longfellow, which no doubt owed much of their fame
to qualities that were less prominent in some of his produc-
tions which perhaps were, not unnaturally, less popular.
. . . But it may be said as a general rule, that when Longfellow was commonplace in sentiment he was far from

commonplace in expression. His verse was full of grace, and, if one may use the word in this connection, of tact; and it cannot perhaps be said to have been want of tact that prevented him from correcting the one odd blunder that he made after it had gone forth to the world and become somewhat surprisingly popular. That he could be and generally was much the reverse of commonplace, will hardly be denied by any one who has made a real study of his work. He had a keen observation, a vivid fancy, a scholarlike touch, a not too common *gentillesse*, and a seemingly easy command of rhyme and rhythm. . . .

When the qualities which we have touched upon are united in a man who has come before the world as a poet, evidently in consequence of the promptings of his nature, and not of malice prepense and with carefully devised affectation, it seems somewhat rash to deny him the high place which the great bulk of his admirers would assign to him, because he has, perhaps too frequently, lapsed into thought, if not into diction, which may seem unworthy of such a writer at his best.

Nor, perhaps, is it fair in this regard to leave out of account that Longfellow began his poetic career as the poet—the poet *par excellence*—of a country which had its literature to make. . . . His position as the spokesman in poetry of a young country had its advantages and its draw backs. He was more free from the disadvantages of critical severity and opposition than an English writer could well have been ; but such a freedom has its dangers, and to this it might not be too fanciful to trace the lapses of which some mention has been made. That it was to these lapses that he owed a considerable portion of his influence with the mass of the reading or devouring public in England was not his fault ; and this fact should not, we think, be allowed to obscure in any way the exceptionally fine qualities which he undoubtedly possessed and cultivated."

—*London Saturday Review.*

THE essence of Longfollow's writings might be defined thus : domestic morals, with a romantic coloring, a warm glow of sentiment, and a full measure of culture. The morals are partly religious, hardly at all sectarian, pure, sincere, and healthy. The romance is sufficiently genuine, yet a trifle factitious, nicely apprehended rather than intense. The sentiment is heart-felt, but a little ordinary— by the very fact of its being ordinary all the more widely and fully responded to—at times with a somewhat false ring, or at least an obvious shallowness ; right-minded sentiment, which the author perceives to be creditable to himself, and which he aims, as if by an earnest and "penetrated" tone of voice, to make impressive to his reader. The culture is broad and general ; not that of a bookworm or student, but of a receptive and communicative mind, of average grasp and average sympathies. . . . Longfellow had much clearness and persuasiveness, some force, and a great aptitude for "improving the occasion ;" but he had not that imaginative strength, that spacious vision, that depth of personal individuality which impress somewhat painfully at first, but which alone supply in the long-run the great startling and rousing forces that possess a permanent influence.—*London Athenæum.*

LONGFELLOW has a perfect command of that expression which results from restraining rather than cultivating fluency ; and his manner is adapted to his theme. He rarely, if ever, mistakes emotions for conceptions. His words are often pictures of his thought. He selects with great delicacy and precision the exact phrase which best expresses or suggests his idea. He colors his style with the skill of a painter. The warm flush and bright tints, as well as the most evanescent hues, of language he uses with admirable discretion. In that higher department of his art, that of so combining his words and images that they make music to the soul as well as to the ear, and convey not only his feelings and thoughts, but also the very tone and condition of

the soul in which they have being, he likewise excels. . . .
. . . His imagination, in the sphere of its activity, is al-
most perfect in its power to shape in visible forms, or to
suggest, by cunning verbal combinations, the feeling or
thought he desires to express ; but it lacks the strength and
daring, and the wide sweep, which characterize the imagination of such poets as Shelley. He has little of the unrest
and frenzy of the bard. We know, in reading him, that he
will never miss his mark ; that he will risk nothing ; that
he will aim to do only that which he feels he can do well.
An air of repose, of quiet power, is around his compositions.
He rarely loses sight of common interests and sympathies.
He displays none of the stinging earnestness, the vehement
sensibility, the gusts of passion, which characterize poets
of the impulsive class. His spiritualism is not seen in wild
struggles after an ineffable Something, for which earth can
afford but imperfect symbols, and of which even abstract
words can suggest little knowledge. He appears perfectly
satisfied with his work. Like his own "Village Blacksmith," he retires every night with the feeling that something has been attempted, that something has been *done*.
. . . His sense of beauty, though uncommonly vivid, is not
the highest of which the mind is capable. He has little
perception of its mysterious spirit ; of that beauty, of which
all physical loveliness is but the shadow, which awes and
thrills the soul into which it enters, and lifts the imagination into regions " to which the heaven of heavens is but a
veil." His mind never appears oppressed, nor his sight
dimmed, by its exceeding glory. He feels and loves, and
creates what is beautiful ; but he hymns no reverence, he
pays no adoration, to the Spirit of Beauty. He would
never exclaim with Shelley, "O awful Loveliness!"—*E. P.
Whipple.*

VOICES OF THE NIGHT

PRELUDE

PLEASANT it was, when woods were green,
   And winds were soft and low,
To lie amid some sylvan scene,
Where, the long drooping boughs between,
Shadows dark and sunlight sheen   5
   Alternate come and go ;

Or where the denser grove receives
   No sunlight from above,
But the dark foliage interweaves
In one unbroken roof of leaves,   10
Underneath whose sloping eaves
   The shadows hardly move.

Beneath some patriarchal tree
   I lay upon the ground ;
His hoary arms uplifted he,   15
And all the broad leaves over me
Clapped their little hands in glee
   With one continuous sound ;—

A slumberous sound,—a sound that brings
   The feelings of a dream,—   20
As of innumerable wings,
As, when a bell no longer swings,
Faint the hollow murmur rings
   O'er meadow, lake, and stream.

13

And dreams of that which cannot die,
   Bright visions, came to me,
As lapped in thought I used to lie,
And gaze into the summer sky.
5   Where the sailing clouds went by,
   Like ships upon the sea ;

Dreams that the soul of youth engage
   Ere Fancy has been quelled ;
Old legends of the monkish page,
10   Traditions of the saint and sage,
Tales that have the rime of age,
   And chronicles of Eld.

And, loving still these quaint old themes,
   Even in the city's throng
15   I feel the freshness of the streams,
That, crossed by shades and sunny gleams,
Water the green land of dreams,
   The holy land of song.

Therefore, at Pentecost, which brings
   The Spring, clothed like a bride,
20   When nestling buds unfold their wings,
And bishop's-caps have golden rings,
Musing upon many things,
   I sought the woodlands wide.

25   The green trees whispered low and mild ;
   It was a sound of joy !
They were my playmates when a child,
And rocked me in their arms so wild !
Still they looked at me and smiled,
30   As if I were a boy ;

---

22. **Bishop's cap.** A plant of the genus Mitella, so called from the shape of its pod. It has a small greenish flower.

And ever whispered, mild and low,
   "Come, be a child once more!"
And waved their long arms to and fro,
And beckoned solemnly and slow ;
O, I could not choose but go   5
   Into the woodlands hoar ;

Into the blithe and breathing air,
   Into the solemn wood,
Solemn and silent everywhere !
Nature with folded hands seemed there,   10
Kneeling at her evening prayer !
   Like one in prayer I stood.

Before me rose an avenue
   Of tall and sombrous pines ;
Abroad their fan-like branches grew,   15
And, where the sunshine darted through,
Spread a vapor soft and blue,
   In long and sloping lines.

And, falling on my weary brain,
   Like a fast-falling shower,   20
The dreams of youth came back again ;
Low lispings of the summer rain,
Dropping on the ripened grain,
   As once upon the flower.

Visions of childhood ! Stay, O stay !   25
   Ye were so sweet and wild !
And distant voices seemed to say,
"It cannot be!   They pass away !
Other themes demand thy lay ;
Thou art no more a child !   30

" The land of Song within thee lies,
Watered by living springs ;
The lids of Fancy's sleepless eyes
Are gates unto that Paradise,
5   Holy thoughts, like stars, arise,
Its clouds are angels' wings.

" Learn, that henceforth thy song shall be,
Not mountains capped with snow,
Nor forests sounding like the sea,
10   Nor rivers flowing carelessly,
Where the woodlands bend to see
The bending heavens below.

" There is a forest where the din
Of iron branches sounds !
15   A mighty river roars between,
And whosoever looks therein
Sees the heavens all black with sin,
Sees not its depths, nor bounds.

" Athwart the swinging branches cast,
20   Soft rays of sunshine pour ;
Then comes the fearful wintry blast ;
Our hopes, like withered leaves, fall fast,
Pallid lips say, ' It is past !
We can return no more ! '

25   " Look, then, into thine heart, and write !
Yes, into Life's deep stream !
All forms of sorrow and delight,
All solemn Voices of the Night,
That can soothe thee, or affright,—
30   Be these henceforth thy theme."

HYMN TO THE NIGHT

Πότνια, πότνια νύξ,
ὑπνοδότειρα τῶν πολυπόνων βροτῶν,
Ἐρεβόθεν ἴθι μόλε μόλε κατάπτερος
Ἀγαμεμνόνιον ἐπὶ δόμον·
ὑπὸ γὰρ ἀλγέων, ὑπό τε συμφορᾶς   5
διοιχόμεθ', οἰχόμεθα.

EURIPIDES.

Ἀσπασίη, τρίλλιστος.

I HEARD the trailing garments of the Night
  Sweep through her marble halls !
I saw her sable skirts all fringed with light   10
  From the celestial walls !

I felt her presence, by its spell of might,
  Stoop o'er me from above ;
The calm, majestic presence of the Night,   15
  As of the one I love.

---

1. πότνια, πότνια νύξ, etc.
  [Awful queen, whose gentle power
    Brings sweet oblivion of our woes,
  And in the calm and gentle hour
    Distils the blessings of repose ;—
      Come, awful Night ;]
  Come from the gloom of Erebus profound,
  And spread thy sable tinctured wings around ;
    Speed to this royal house thy flight ;
    For pale-eyed Grief, and wild Affright,
    And all the horrors of Despair,___...
  Here pour their rage, and threaten ruin here.
      Euripides' *Orestes*, 178-188, tr. by R. POTTER.
8. Ἀσπασίη, τρίλλιστος . . . νύξ—most welcome, earnestly prayed for night. *Iliad*, 8, 488.

2

I heard the sounds of sorrow and delight,
　　The manifold, soft chimes,
That fill the haunted chambers of the Night,
　　Like some old poet's Rhymes.

5　　From the cool cisterns of the midnight air
　　　My spirit drank repose ;
The fountain of perpetual peace flows there,—
　　From those deep cisterns flows.

O holy Night ! from thee I learn to bear
10　　What man has borne before !
Thou layest thy finger on the lips of Care,
　　And they complain no more.

Peace ! Peace ! Orestes-like I breathe this prayer !
　　Descend with broad-winged flight,
15　　The welcome, the thrice-prayed for, the most fair,
　　The best beloved Night !

———

A PSALM OF LIFE

WHAT THE HEART OF THE YOUNG MAN SAID TO
THE PSALMIST.

TELL me not, in mournful numbers,
　　" Life is but an empty dream ! "
For the soul is dead that slumbers,
20　　And things are not what they seem.

---

13. **Orestes.** In classic mythology a son of Agamemnon and Clytemnestra ; he was pursued by the Furies, who drove him mad as a punishment for the murder of his mother. In the tragedy " Orestes " by Euripides, Orestes calls on sleep as his greatest boon.

Life is real!   Life is earnest!
  And the grave is not its goal ;
" Dust thou art, to dust returnest,"
  Was not spoken of the soul.

Not enjoyment, and not sorrow,
  Is our destined end or way ;
But to act, that each to-morrow
  Find us farther than to-day.

Art is long, and Time is fleeting,
  And our hearts, though stout and brave,
Still, like muffled drums, are beating
  Funeral marches to the grave.

In the world's broad field of battle,
  In the bivouac of Life,
Be not like dumb, driven cattle !
  Be a hero in the strife !

Trust no Future, howe'er pleasant !
  Let the dead past bury its dead !
Act,—act in the living Present !
  Heart within, and God o'erhead !

Lives of great men all remind us
  We can make our lives sublime,
And, departing, leave behind us
  Footsteps on the sands of time ;—

3. "Dust thou art, to dust returnest." Genesis iii. 19.
9. Art is long, and time is fleeting. Compare: "Ars longa, vita brevis" (art is long, time short)—Hippocrates, Aphorism I.; "The lyfe so short, the craft so long to learn"—Chaucer's *The Assembly of Fowles*; "Die Kunst ist lang, das Leben kurz "—Göthe's *Wilhelm Meister*, vii. 9.
24. Footsteps. In later editions Longfellow changed this to "footprints."

Footsteps, that perhaps another,
  Sailing o'er life's solemn main,
A forlorn and shipwrecked brother,
  Seeing, shall take heart again.

5   Let us, then, be up and doing,
      With a heart for any fate ;
    Still achieving, still pursuing,
      Learn to labor and to wait.

———

THE REAPER AND THE FLOWERS

THERE is a Reaper, whose name is Death,
10   And, with his sickle keen,
    He reaps the bearded grain at a breath,
      And the flowers that grow between.

    " Shall I have nought that is fair ? " saith he ;
      " Have nought but the bearded grain ?
15   Though the breath of these flowers is sweet to me,
      I will give them all back again."

    He gazed at the flowers with tearful eyes,
      He kissed their drooping leaves ;
    It was for the Lord of Paradise
20   He bound them in his sheaves.

    " My Lord has need of these flowerets gay,"
      The Reaper said, and smiled ;
    " Dear tokens of the earth are they,
      Where he was once a child.

" They shall all bloom in fields of light,
    Transplanted by my care,
And saints, upon their garments white,
    These sacred blossoms wear."

And the mother gave, in tears and pain,   5
    The flowers she most did love ;
She knew she should find them all again
    In the fields of light above.

O, not in cruelty, not in wrath,
    The Reaper came that day ;   10
'T was an angel visited the green earth,
    And took the flowers away.

THE LIGHT OF STARS

THE night is come, but not too soon ;
    And sinking silently,
All silently, the little moon   15
    Drops down behind the sky.

There is no light in earth or heaven
    But the cold light of stars ;
And the first watch of night is given
    To the red planet Mars.   20

Is it the tender star of love ?
    The star of love and dreams ?
O no ! from that blue tent above,
    A hero's armor gleams.

---

20. **The red planet Mars.** Mars shines with a fiery red light, probably
caused by the redness of its soil.

And earnest thoughts within me rise,
 When I behold afar,
Suspended in the evening skies,
 The shield of that red star.

5 O star of strength ! I see thee stand
 And smile upon my pain ;
Thou beckonest with thy mailed hand,
 And I am strong again.

Within my breast there is no light,
10 But the cold light of stars ;
I give the first watch of the night
 To the red planet Mars.

The star of the unconquered will,
 He rises in my breast,
15 Serene, and resolute, and still,
 And calm, and self-possessed.

And thou, too, whosoe'er thou art,
 That readest this brief psalm,
As one by one thy hopes depart,
20 Be resolute and calm.

O fear not in a world like this,
 And thou shalt know ere long,
Know how sublime a thing it is
 To suffer and be strong.

FOOTSTEPS OF ANGELS

25 WHEN the hours of Day are numbered,
 And the voices of the Night
Wake the better soul, that slumbered,
 To a holy, calm delight ;

Ere the evening lamps are lighted,
  And, like phantoms grim and tall,
Shadows from the fitful fire-light
  Dance upon the parlor wall;

Then the forms of the departed   5
  Enter at the open door;
The beloved, the true-hearted,
  Come to visit me once more;

He, the young and strong, who cherished
  Noble longings for the strife,   10
By the road-side fell and perished,
  Weary with the march of life!

They, the holy ones and weakly,
  Who the cross of suffering bore,
Folded their pale hands so meekly,   15
  Spake with us on earth no more!

And with them the Being Beauteous,
  Who unto my youth was given,
More than all things else to love me,
  And is now a saint in heaven.   20

With a slow and noiseless footstep
  Comes that messenger divine,
Takes the vacant chair beside me,
  Lays her gentle hand in mine.

And she sits and gazes at me   25
  With those deep and tender eyes,
Like the stars, so still and saint-like,
  Looking downward from the skies.

---

17. **Being beauteous.** An allusion to his first wife.

Uttered not, yet comprehended,
   Is the spirit's voiceless prayer,
Soft rebukes, in blessings ended,
   Breathing from her lips of air.

5   O, though oft depressed and lonely,
   All my fears are laid aside,
If I but remember only
   Such as these have lived and died !

―――――

FLOWERS

SPAKE full well, in language quaint and olden,
10   One who dwelleth by the castled Rhine,
When he called the flowers, so blue and golden,
   Stars, that in earth's firmament do shine.

Stars they are, wherein we read our history,
   As astrologers and seers of eld ;
15 Yet not wrapped about with awful mystery,
   Like the burning stars, which they beheld.

Wondrous truths, and manifold as wondrous,
   God hath written in those stars above ;
But not less in the bright flowerets under us
20   Stands the revelation of his love.

Bright and glorious is that revelation,
   Written all over this great world of ours ;
Making evident our own creation,
   In these stars of earth,—these golden flowers.

―――――――――――――――――――――――――――――

10. **One who dwelleth.** He who thus spake so well was Carové in his
Story without an End.

And the Poet, faithful and far-seeing,
    Sees, alike in stars and flowers, a part
Of the self-same, universal being,
    Which is throbbing in his brain and heart.

Gorgeous flowerets in the sunlight shining,   5
    Blossoms flaunting in the eye of day,
Tremulous leaves, with soft and silver lining,
    Buds that open only to decay ;

Brilliant hopes, all woven in gorgeous tissues,
    Flaunting gayly in the golden light ;   10
Large desires, with most uncertain issues,
    Tender wishes, blossoming at night !

These in flowers and men are more than seeming ;
    Workings are they of the self-same powers ;
Which the Poet, in no idle dreaming,   15
    Seeth in himself and in the flowers.

Everywhere about us are they glowing,
    Some like stars, to tell us Spring is born ;
Others, their blue eyes with tears o'erflowing,
    Stand like Ruth amid the golden corn ;   20

Not alone in Spring's armorial bearing,
    And in Summer's green-emblazoned field,
But in arms of brave old Autumn's wearing,
    In the centre of his brazen shield ;

Not alone in meadows and green alleys,   25
    On the mountain-top, and by the brink
Of sequestered pools in woodland valleys,
    Where the slaves of Nature stoop to drink ;

---

20 **Ruth amid the golden corn.** Ruth ii. 3.

Not alone in her vast dome of glory,
  . Not on graves of bird and beast alone,
But in old cathedrals, high and hoary,
    On the tombs of heroes, carved in stone ;

5 In the cottage of the rudest peasant,
      In ancestral homes, whose crumbling towers,
Speaking of the Past unto the Present,
      Tell us of the ancient Games of Flowers ;

In all places, then, and in all seasons,
10   Flowers expand their light and soul-like wings,
Teaching us, by most persuasive reasons,
      How akin they are to human things.

And with childlike, credulous affection
    We behold their tender buds expand ;
15 Emblems of our own great resurrection,
    Emblems of the bright and better land

THE BELEAGUERED CITY

I HAVE read, in some old marvellous tale,
    Some legend strange and vague,
That a midnight host of spectres pale
20   Beleaguered the walls of Prague.

Beside the Moldau's rushing stream,
    With the wan moon overhead,
There stood, as in an awful dream,
    The army of the dead.

25   White as a sea-fog, landward bound,
    The spectral camp was seen,
And, with a sorrowful, deep sound,
    The river flowed between.

No other voice nor sound was there,
   No drum, nor sentry's pace ;
The mist-like banners clasped the air,
   As clouds with clouds embrace.

But, when the old cathedral bell   5
   Proclaimed the morning prayer,
The white pavilions rose and fell
   On the alarmed air.

Down the broad valley fast and far
   The troubled army fled ;   10
Up rose the glorious morning star,
   The ghastly host was dead.

I have read, in the marvellous heart of man,
   That strange and mystic scroll,
That an army of phantoms vast and wan   15
   Beleaguer the human soul.

Encamped beside Life's rushing stream,
   In Fancy's misty light,
Gigantic shapes and shadows gleam
   Portentous through the night.   20

Upon its midnight battle-ground
   The spectral camp is seen,
And, with a sorrowful, deep sound,
   Flows the River of Life between.

No other voice, nor sound is there,   25
   In the army of the grave ;
No other challenge breaks the air,
   But the rushing of Life's wave.

And, when the solemn and deep church-bell
    Entreats the soul to pray,
The midnight phantoms feel the spell,
    The shadows sweep away.

5   Down the broad Vale of Tears afar
       The spectral camp is fled ;
    Faith shineth **as** a morning star,
       Our ghastly fears are dead.

——————

MIDNIGHT MASS FOR THE DYING YEAR

Yes, the Year is growing old,
10   And his eye is pale and bleared !
Death, with frosty hand and cold,
    Plucks the old man by the beard,
       Sorely,—sorely !

The leaves are falling, falling,
15   Solemnly and slow ;
"Caw ! caw !" the rooks are calling,
    It is a sound of woe,
       A sound of woe !

Through the woods and mountain passes
20   The winds, like anthems, roll ;
They are chanting solemn masses,
    Singing : " Pray for this poor soul,
       Pray,—pray ! "

And the hooded clouds, like friars,
25   Tell their beads in drops of rain,
And patter their doleful prayers ;—
    But their prayers are all in vain,
       All in vain !

There he stands in the foul weather,
  The foolish, fond Old Year,
Crowned with wild flowers and with heather,
  Like weak, despised Lear,
    A king,—a king ;   5

Then comes the summer-like day,
  Bids the old man rejoice !
His joy ! his last ! O, the old man gray
  Loveth that ever-soft voice,
    Gentle and low.   10

To the crimson woods he saith,—
  To the voice gentle and low
Of the soft air, like a daughter's breath,—
  "Pray do not mock me so !
    Do not laugh at me ! "   15

And now the sweet day is dead ;
  Cold in his arms it lies ;
No stain from its breath is spread
  Over the glassy skies,
    No mist or stain !   20

Then, too, the Old Year dieth,
  And the forests utter a moan,
Like the voice of one who crieth
  In the wilderness alone,
    "Vex not his ghost ! "   25

---

4. **Weak, despised Lear.** Lear, mythical king of Britain, at the age of fourscore resolved to divide his kingdom among his three daughters in proportion to their love. The two eldest said they loved him more than tongue could express, but the youngest said she loved him as it became a daughter to love her father. This answer of his youngest daughter displeased the old king and he disinherited her. When the elder daughters were put to the test, however, they proved ungrateful and treated their father with scant courtesy, while the youngest showed herself loving and true. Shakespeare's *King Lear*.

Then comes, with an awful roar,
    Gathering and sounding on,
The storm-wind from Labrador,
    The wind Euroclydon,
5   The storm-wind !

Howl ! howl ! and from the forest
    Sweep the red leaves away !
Would the sins that thou abhorrest,
    O Soul ! could thus decay,
10   And be swept away !

For there shall come a mightier blast,
    There shall be a darker day ;
And the stars, from heaven downcast,
    Like red leaves be swept away !
15   Kyrie, eleyson !
        Christe, eleyson !

---

4. **Euroclydon.** A tempestuous southeast wind, which raises great waves. The name is derived from the Greek *euros*, the southeast wind and *klydon*, a wave.

15. **Kyrie, Eleyson ! Christe, Eleyson.** In Greek, "Lord have pity, Christ have pity." Brief petitions used as responses in the Roman Catholic Church.

MISCELLANEOUS

THE SKELETON IN ARMOR

[The following Ballad was suggested to me while riding on the seashore at Newport. A year or two previous a skeleton had been dug up at Fall River, clad in broken and corroded armor; and the idea occurred to me of connecting it with the Round Tower at Newport, generally known hitherto as the Old Wind-Mill, though now claimed by the Danes as a work of their early ancestors. Professor Rafn, in the *Mémoires de la Société Royale des Antiquaires du Nord*, for 1838–1839, says:

"There is no mistaking in this instance the style in which the more ancient stone edifices of the North were constructed, the style which belongs to the Roman or Ante-Gothic architecture, and which, especially after the time of Charlemagne, diffused itself from Italy over the whole of the West and North of Europe, where it continued to predominate until the close of the 12th century; that style, which some authors have, from one of its most striking characteristics, called the round arch style, the same which in England is denominated Saxon and sometimes Norman architecture.

"On the ancient structure in Newport there are no ornaments remaining, which might possibly have served to guide us in assigning the probable date of its erection. That no vestige whatever is found of the pointed arch, nor any approximation to it, is indicative of an earlier rather than of a later period. From such characteristics as remain, however, we can scarcely form any other inference than one, in which I am persuaded that all, who are familiar with Old-Northern architecture, will concur, THAT THIS BUILDING WAS ERECTED AT A PERIOD DECIDEDLY NOT LATER THAN THE 12TH CENTURY. This remark applies, of course, to the original building only, and not to the alterations that it subsequently received; for there are several such alterations in the upper part of the building which cannot be mistaken, and which were most likely occasioned by its being adapted in modern times to various uses, for example as the substructure of a wind-mill, and latterly as a hay magazine. To the same times may be referred the windows, the fireplace, and the apertures made above the columns. That this building could not have been erected for a wind-mill, is what an architect will easily discern."

I will not enter into a discussion of the point. It is sufficiently well established for the purpose of a ballad; though doubtless many an honest citizen of Newport, who has passed his days within sight of the Round Tower, will be ready to exclaim with Sancho : "God bless me ! did I not warn you to have a care of what you were doing, for that it was nothing but a wind-mill ; and nobody could mistake it, but one who had the like in his head."

"SPEAK ! speak ! thou fearful guest !
Who, with thy hollow breast
Still in rude armor drest,
    Comest to daunt me !
Wrapt not in Eastern balms,
But with thy fleshless palms
Stretched, as if asking alms,
    Why dost thou haunt me ?"

Then, from those cavernous eyes
Pale flashes seemed to rise,
As when the Northern skies
    Gleam in December ;
And, like the water's flow
Under December's snow,
Came a dull voice of woe
    From the heart's chamber.

---

5. **Eastern balms.** In ancient Egypt and in other Eastern countries, it was common to embalm the bodies of the dead with spices and various aromatic substances.

11. **Northern skies.** The aurora borealis, or streams of light that appear in the northern sky in winter, is probably caused by the passage of electricity through the upper regions of the air, though under conditions not as yet entirely understood.

" I was a Viking old !
My deeds, though manifold,
No Skald in song has told,
    No Saga taught thee !
Take heed, that in thy verse   5
Thou dost the tale rehearse,
Else dread a dead man's curse !
    For this I sought thee.

" Far in the Northern land,
By the wild Baltic's strand,   10
I, with my childish hand,
    Tamed the ger-falcon ;
And, with my skates fast-bound,
Skimmed the half-frozen Sound,
That the poor whimpering hound   15
    Trembled to walk on.

" Oft to his frozen lair
Tracked I the grisly bear,
While from my path the hare
    Fled like a shadow ;   20
Oft through the forest dark
Followed the were-wolf's bark,
Until the soaring lark
    Sang from the meadow.

---

3. **Skald.** The Skalds were the ancient Scandinavian minstrels who composed poems in honor of distinguished men and sang them on public occasions.

4. **Saga.** The long legends or tales of mythological or historical events which formed the literature of the ancient Norsemen.

12. **Ger-falcon.** The large falcon of northern Europe, in great demand for the sport of hawking. *Ger* comes from the same root as the German *gierig*, eager, greedy.

22. **Were-wolf.** A human being turned into a wolf while retaining human intelligence. The transformation could be voluntarily made by

3

"But when I older grew,
Joining a corsair's crew,
O'er the dark sea I flew
    With the marauders.
5   Wild was the life we led ;
Many the souls that sped,
Many the hearts that bled,
    By our stern orders.

"Many a wassail-bout
10   Wore the long Winter out ;
Often our midnight shout
    Set the cocks crowing,
As we the Berserk's tale
Measured in cups of ale,
15   Draining the oaken pail,
    Filled to o'erflowing.

"Once as I told in glee
Tales of the stormy sea,
Soft eyes did gaze on me,
20   Burning yet tender ;
And as the white stars shine
On the dark Norway pine,
On that dark heart of mine
    Fell their soft splendor.

25   "I wooed the blue-eyed maid,
Yielding, yet half afraid,

---

infernal aid or by witchcraft. Men were tried on the charge of being were-wolves as late as the seventeenth century. The superstition still exists in certain parts of Europe where wolves abound. From the Anglo-Saxon *wer*, man and wolf, a man-wolf, literally.

13. **Berserk.** Berserker was a redoubtable hero in Scandinavian mythology who had twelve sons who inherited the battle frenzy or berserker rage. The sagas are full of tales of heroes who are seized with this fierce longing for carnage. The name means *bear shirt*.

And in the forest's shade
   Our vows were plighted.
Under its loosened vest
Fluttered her little breast,
Like birds within their nest   5
   By the hawk frighted.

" Bright in her father's hall
Shields gleamed upon the wall,
Loud sang the minstrels all,
   Chanting his glory ;   10
When of old Hildebrand
I asked his daughter's hand,
Mute did the minstrels stand
   To hear my story.

" While the brown ale he quaffed,   15
Loud then the champion laughed,
And as the wind-gusts waft
   The sea-foam brightly,
So the loud laugh of scorn,
Out of those lips unshorn,   20
From the deep drinking-horn
   Blew the foam lightly.

" She was a Prince's child,
I but a Viking wild,
And though she blushed and smiled,   25
   I was discarded !
Should not the dove so white
Follow the sea-mew's flight,
Why did they leave that night
   Her nest unguarded ?   30

"Scarce had I put to sea,
   Bearing the maid with me,—
   Fairest of all was she
      Among the Norsemen!—
5 When on the white sea-strand,
   Waving his armèd hand,
   Saw we old Hildebrand,
      With twenty horsemen.

   "Then launched they to the blast,
10 Bent like a reed each mast,
   Yet we were gaining fast,
      When the wind failed us;
   And with a sudden flaw
   Came round the gusty Skaw,
15 So that our foe we saw
      Laugh as he hailed us.

   " And as to catch the gale
   Round veered the flapping sail,
   Death! was the helmsman's hail,
20   Death without quarter!
   Mid-ships with iron keel
   Struck we her ribs of steel;
   Down her black hulk did reel
      Through the black water!

25 " As with his wings aslant,
   Sails the fierce cormorant,
   Seeking some rocky haunt,
      With his prey laden,

---

14. **Skaw.** A word of Icelandic extraction meaning headland.

So toward the open main,
Beating to sea again,
Through the wild hurricane,
   Bore I the maiden.

"Three weeks we westward bore,   5
And when the storm was o'er,
Cloud-like we saw the shore
   Stretching to lee-ward ;
There for my lady's bower
Built I the lofty tower,   10
Which, to this very hour,
   Stands looking sea-ward.

"There lived we many years ;
Time dried the maiden's tears ;
She had forgot her fears,   15
   She was a mother ;
Death closed her mild blue eyes,
Under that tower she lies ;
Ne'er shall the sun arise
   On such another !   20

"Still grew my bosom then,
Still as a stagnant fen !
Hateful to me were men,
   The sunlight hateful !
In the vast forest here,   25
Clad in my warlike gear,
Fell I upon my spear,
   O, death was grateful !

"Thus, seamed with many scars,
Bursting these prison bars,   30
Up to its native stars
   My soul ascended !

There from the flowing bowl
Deep drinks the warrior's soul,
Skoal! to the Northland! *skoal!*"
—Thus the tale ended.

THE WRECK OF THE HESPERUS

5   IT was the schooner Hesperus,
       That sailed the wintry sea;
     And the skipper had taken his little daughter
       To bear him company.

     Blue were her eyes as the fairy-flax,
10   Her cheeks like the dawn of day,
     And her bosom white as the hawthorn buds,
       That ope in the month of May.

     The skipper he stood beside the helm,
       With his pipe in his mouth,
15   And watched how the veering flaw did blow
       The smoke now West, now South.

     Then up and spake an old Sailòr,
       Had sailed the Spanish Main,
     "I pray thee, put into yonder port,
20   For I fear a hurricane.

---

3. **Skoal.** "In Scandinavia this is the customary salutation when drinking a health. I have slightly changed the orthography of the word, in order to preserve the correct pronunciation." *Author's note.*

18. **Spanish Main.** The northeast coast of South America, between the Orinoco River and the Isthmus of Panama, and the adjoining part of the Caribbean Sea. The Spanish main used to be a favorite haunt of pirates.

" Last night, the moon had a golden ring,
 And to-night no moon we see ! "
The skipper, he blew a whiff from his pipe,
 And a scornful laugh laughed he.

Colder and louder blew the wind,   5
 A gale from the Northeast ;
The snow fell hissing in the brine,
 And the billows frothed like yeast.

Down came the storm, and smote amain,
 The vessel in its strength ;   10
She shuddered and paused, like a frightened steed,
 Then leaped her cable's length.

"Come hither ! come hither ! my little daughtèr,
 And do not tremble so ;
For I can weather the roughest gale,   15
 That ever wind did blow."

He wrapped her warm in his seaman's coat,
 Against the stinging blast ;
He cut a rope from a broken spar
 And bound her to the mast.   20

"O father ! I hear the church-bells ring,
 O say, what may it be ? "
 'T is a fog-bell on a rock-bound coast ! "
 And he steered for the open sea.

" O father ! I hear the sound of guns, 25
 O say, what may it be ? "
" Some ship in distress that cannot live
 In such an angry sea ! "

"O father ! I see a gleaming light,
    O say, what may it be ?"
But the father answered never a word,
    A frozen corpse was he.

5 Lashed to the helm, all stiff and stark,
      With his face to the skies,
   The lantern gleamed through the gleaming snow
      On his fixed and glassy eyes.

   Then the maiden clasped her hands and prayed
10   That savèd she might be ;
   And she thought of Christ who stilled the wave,
      On the Lake of Galilee.

   And fast through the midnight dark and drear,
      Through the whistling sleet and snow,
15 Like a sheeted ghost, the vessel swept
      Towards the reef of Norman's Woe.

   And ever the fitful gusts between
      A sound came from the land ;
   It was the sound of the trampling surf,
20   On the rocks and the hard sea-sand.

   The breakers were right beneath her bows,
      She drifted a dreary wreck,
   And a whooping billow swept the crew
      Like icicles from her deck.

25 She struck where the white and fleecy waves
      Looked soft as carded wool,
   But the cruel rocks, they gored her side
      Like the horns of an angry bull.

Her rattling shrouds, all sheathed in ice,
  With the masts went by the board ;
Like a vessel of glass, she strove and sank.
  Ho ! ho !   the breakers roared !

At daybreak, on the bleak sea-beach,   5
  A fisherman stood aghast,
To see the form of a maiden fair,
  Lashed close to a drifting mast.

The salt sea was frozen on her breast,
  The salt tears in her eyes ;   10
And he saw her hair, like the brown sea-weed,
  On the billows fall and rise.

Such was the wreck of the Hesperus,
  In the midnight and the snow !
Christ save us all from a death like this,   15
  On the reef of Norman's Woe !

THE LUCK OF EDENHALL

FROM THE GERMAN OF UHLAND.

[The tradition, upon which this ballad is founded, and the
"shards of the Luck of Edenhall," still exist in England.   The
goblet is in the possession of Sir Christopher Musgrave, Bart.,
of Eden Hall, Cumberland ; and is not so entirely shattered,
as the ballad leaves it.]

OF Edenhall, the youthful Lord
  Bids sound the festal trumpet's call ;
He rises at the banquet board,

---

16. **Norman's Woe.**   A dangerous reef at the entrance to the harbor of
Gloucester, Massachusetts.   A schooner called the Hesperus actually went
to pieces on the rocks here in the winter of 1839.   Longfellow heard of it in
a newspaper and composed the famous balled in a single night.

And cries, 'mid the drunken revellers all,
" Now bring me the Luck of Edenhall ! "

The butler hears the words with pain,
The house's oldest seneschal,
5   Takes slow from its silken cloth again
The drinking glass of crystal tall ;
They call it the Luck of Edenhall.

Then said the Lord : " This glass to praise,
Fill with red wine from Portugal ! "
10   The gray-beard with trembling hand obeys ;
A purple light shines over all,
It beams from the Luck of Edenhall.

Then speaks the Lord, and waves it light,
" This glass of flashing crystal tall
15   Gave to my sires the Fountain-Sprite ;
She wrote in it : *If this glass doth fall,*
Farewell then, O Luck of Edenhall !

" 'T was right a goblet the Fate should be
Of the joyous race of Edenhall !
20   Deep draughts drink we right willingly ;
And willingly ring, with merry call,
Kling ! klang ! to the Luck of Edenhall ! "

First rings it deep, and full, and mild,
Like to the song of a nightingale ;
25   Then like the roar of a torrent wild ;
Then mutters at last like the thunder's fall,
The glorious Luck of Edenhall.

" For its keeper takes a race of might,
The fragile goblet of crystal tall ;

It has lasted longer than is right ;
Kling ! klang !—with a harder blow than all
Will I try the Luck of Edenhall ! "

As the goblet ringing flies apart,
Suddenly cracks the vaulted hall ;   5
And through the rift, the wild flames start ;
The guests in dust are scattered all ;
With the breaking Luck of Edenhall !

In storms the foe, with fire and sword ;
He in the night had scaled the wall,   10
Slain by the sword lies the youthful Lord,
But holds in his hand the crystal tall,
The shattered Luck of Edenhall.

On the morrow the butler gropes alone,
The gray-beard in the desert hall,   15
He seeks his Lord's burnt skeleton,
He seeks in the dismal ruin's fall
The shards of the Luck of Edenhall.

" The stone wall," saith he, " doth fall aside,
Down must the stately columns fall ;   20
Glass is this earth's Luck and Pride ;
In atoms shall fall this earthly ball
One day like the Luck of Edenhall ! "

THE ELECTED KNIGHT

FROM THE DANISH.

[The following strange and somewhat mystical ballad is
from Nyerup and Rahbek's *Danske Viser* of the Middle Ages.
It seems to refer to the first preaching of Christianity in the
North, and to the institution of Knight-Errantry. The three
maidens I suppose to be Faith, Hope, and Charity. The
irregularities of the original have been carefully preserved in
the translation.]

SIR OLUF he rideth over the plain,
    Full seven miles broad and seven miles wide,
But never, ah never can meet with the man
    A tilt with him dare ride.

5   He saw under the hill-side
    A Knight full well equipped ;
His steed was black, his helm was barred ;
    He was riding at full speed.

He wore upon his spurs
10   Twelve little golden birds ;
Anon he spurred his steed with a clang,
    And there sat all the birds and sang.

He wore upon his mail
    Twelve little golden wheels ;
15   Anon in eddies the wild wind blew,
    And round and round the wheels they flew.

He wore before his breast
    A lance that was poised in rest ;
And it was sharper than diamond-stone,
20   It made Sir Oluf's heart to groan.

He wore upon his helm,
  A wreath of ruddy gold ;
And that gave him the Maidens Three,
  The youngest was fair to behold.

Sir Oluf questioned the Knight eftsoon   5
  If he were come from heaven down ;
" Art thou Christ of Heaven," quoth he,
  " So will I yield me unto thee."

" I am not Christ the Great,
  Thou shalt not yield thee yet ;   10
I am an unknown Knight,
  Three modest Maidens have me bedight."

" Art thou a Knight elected,
  And have three Maidens thee bedight ;
So shalt thou ride a tilt this day,   15
  For all the Maidens' honor ! "

The first tilt they together rode
  They put their steeds to the test ;
The second tilt they together rode,
  They proved their manhood best.   20

The third tilt they together rode,
  Neither of them would yield ;
The fourth tilt they together rode,
  They both fell on the field.

Now lie the lords upon the plain,   25
  And their blood runs unto death ;
Now sit the Maidens in the high tower,
  The youngest sorrows till death.

THE VILLAGE BLACKSMITH

UNDER a spreading chestnut tree
  The village smithy stands ;
The smith, a mighty man is he,
  With large and sinewy hands ;
5 And the muscles of his brawny arms
  Are strong as iron bands.

His hair is crisp, and black, and long,
  His face is like the tan ;
His brow is wet with honest sweat,
10 He earns whate'er he can,
And looks the whole world in the face,
  For he owes not any man.

Week in, week out, from morn till night,
  You can hear his bellows blow ;
15 You can hear him swing his heavy sledge,
  With measured beat and slow,
Like a sexton ringing the village bell,
  When the evening sun is low.

And children coming home from school
20 Look in at the open door ;
They love to see the flaming forge,
  And hear the bellows roar,
And catch the burning sparks that fly
  Like chaff from a threshing floor.

25 He goes on Sunday to the church,
  And sits among his boys ;
He hears the parson pray and preach,
  He hears his daughter's voice

Singing in the village choir,
    And it makes his heart rejoice.

It sounds to him like her mother's voice,
    Singing in Paradise !
He needs must think of her once more,   5
    How in the grave she lies ;
And with his hard, rough hand he wipes
    A tear out of his eyes.

Toiling,—rejoicing,—sorrowing,
    Onward through life he goes ;   10
Each morning sees some task begin,
    Each evening sees it close ;
Something attempted, something done,
    Has earned a night's repose.

Thanks, thanks to thee, my worthy friend,   15
    For the lesson thou hast taught !
Thus at the flaming forge of life
    Our fortunes must be wrought ;
Thus on its sounding anvil shaped
    Each burning deed and thought !   20

ENDYMION

THE rising moon has hid the stars ;
Her level rays, like golden bars,
    Lie on the landscape green,
    With shadows brown between,

5   And silver white the river gleams,
       As if Diana, in her dreams,
          Had dropt her silver bow
          Upon the meadows low.

       On such a tranquil night as this,
10   She woke Endymion with a kiss,
          When, sleeping in the grove,
          He dreamed not of her love.

       Like Dian's kiss, unasked, unsought,
       Love gives itself, but is not bought ;
15   Nor voice, nor sound betrays
       Its deep, impassioned gaze.

       It comes,—the beautiful, the free,
       The crown of all humanity,—
          In silence and alone
20   To seek the elected one.

---

10. **Endymion.** In classic mythology Endymion was a beautiful youth who, while sleeping on Mount Latmus, was seen by the Moon Goddess Diana, whose cold heart was so warmed by his beauty that she came to him and kissed him. The story is a personification of the moon sinking down behind the mountains.

It lifts the boughs, whose shadows deep
Are Life's oblivion, the soul's sleep,
    And kisses the closed eyes
    Of him, who slumbering lies.

O, weary hearts ! O, slumbering eyes !   5
O, drooping souls, whose destinies
    Are fraught with fear and pain,
    Ye shall be loved again !

No one is so accursed by fate,
No one so utterly desolate,   10
    But some heart, though unknown,
    Responds unto his own.

Responds,—as if with unseen wings,
An angel touched its quivering strings ;
    And whispers, in its song,   15
    " Where hast thou stayed so long ? "

THE TWO LOCKS OF HAIR

FROM THE GERMAN OF PFIZER.

A YOUTH, light-hearted and content,
    I wander through the world ;
Here, Arab-like, is pitched my tent
    And straight again is furled.   20

Yet oft I dream, that once a wife
    Close in my heart was locked,
And in the sweet repose of life
    A blessed child I rocked.

4

I wake.   Away that dream,—away !
   Too long did it remain !
So long, that both by night and day
   It ever comes again.

5   The end lies ever in my thought ;
   To a grave so cold and deep
The mother beautiful was brought ;
   Then dropt the child asleep.

But now the dream is wholly o'er,
10   I bathe mine eyes and see ;
And wander through the world once more,
   A youth so light and free.

Two locks,—and they are wondrous fair,—
   Left me that vision mild ;
15   The brown is from the mother's hair,
   The blond is from the child.

And when I see that lock of gold,
   Pale grows the evening-red ;
And when the dark lock I behold,
20   I wish that I were dead.

———

IT IS NOT ALWAYS MAY

No hay pájaros en los nidos de antaño.
                    Spanish Proverb.

THE sun is bright,—the air is clear,
   The darting swallows soar and sing,
And from the stately elms I hear
   The blue-bird prophesying Spring.

———

21.   **No hay pájaros en los nidos de antaño.**   For translation see
last line of third stanza.

So blue yon winding river flows,
  It seems an outlet from the sky,
Where waiting till the west wind blows,
  The freighted clouds at anchor lie.

All things are new ;—the buds, the leaves,   5
  That gild the elm-tree's nodding crest,
And even the nest beneath the eaves ;—
  There are no birds in last year's nest !

All things rejoice in youth and love,
  The fulness of their first delight !   10
And learn from the soft heavens above
  The melting tenderness of night.

Maiden, that read'st this simple rhyme,
  Enjoy thy youth, it will not stay ;
Enjoy the fragments of thy prime,   15
  For O ! it is not always May !

Enjoy the Spring of Love and Youth,
  To some good angel leave the rest ;
For Time will teach thee soon the truth,
  There are no birds in last year's nest !   20

THE RAINY DAY

THE day is cold, and dark, and dreary ;
It rains, and the wind is never weary ;
The vine still clings to the mouldering wall,
But at every gust the dead leaves fall,
  And the day is dark and dreary.   25

---

4. **Freighted clouds.** Longfellow was fond of comparing clouds to ships. Compare the fifth stanza of the Prelude to *Voices of the Night*.

My life is cold, and dark, and dreary ;
It rains, and the wind is never weary ;
My thoughts still cling to the mouldering Past,
But the hopes of youth fall thick in the blast,
5   And the days are dark and dreary.

Be still, sad heart ! and cease repining ;
Behind the clouds is the sun still shining ;
Thy fate is the common fate of all,
Into each life some rain must fall,
10   Some days must be dark and dreary.

GOD'S-ACRE

I LIKE that ancient Saxon phrase, which calls
The burial-ground God's-Acre ! It is just ;
It consecrates each grave within its walls,
And breathes a benison o'er the sleeping dust.

15 God's-Acre ! Yes, that blessed name imparts
Comfort to those, who in the grave have sown
The seed, that they had garnered in their hearts,
Their bread of life, alas ! no more their own.

Into its furrows shall we all be cast,
20   In the sure faith that we shall rise again
At the great harvest, when the archangel's blast
Shall winnow, like a fan, the chaff and grain.

Then shall the good stand in immortal bloom,
In the fair gardens of that second birth ;
25 And each bright blossom, mingle its perfume
With that of flowers, which never bloomed on earth.

With thy rude ploughshare, Death, turn up the sod,
  And spread the furrow for the seed we sow ;
This is the field and Acre of our God,
  This is the place, where human harvests grow !

TO THE RIVER CHARLES

RIVER ! that in silence windest   5
  Through the meadows, bright and free,
Till at length thy rest thou findest
  In the bosom of the sea !

Four long years of mingled feeling,
  Half in rest, and half in strife,   10
I have seen thy waters stealing
  Onward, like the stream of life.

Thou hast taught me, Silent River !
  Many a lesson, deep and long ;
Thou hast been a generous giver ;   15
  I can give thee but a song.

Oft in sadness and in illness,
  I have watched thy current glide,
Till the beauty of its stillness
  Overflowed me, like a tide.   20

And in better hours and brighter,
  When I saw thy waters gleam,
I have felt my heart beat lighter,
  And leap onward with thy stream.

5. **River Charles.** Craigie House, Longfellow's home in Cambridge,
overlooked the Charles River.

Not for this alone I love thee,
　Nor because thy waves of blue
From celestial seas above thee
　Take their own celestial hue.

5　Where yon shadowy woodlands hide thee,
　And thy waters disappear,
Friends I love have dwelt beside thee,
　And have made thy margin dear.

More than this ;—thy name reminds me
10　Of three friends, all true and tried ;
And that name, like magic, binds me
　Closer, closer to thy side.

Friends my soul with joy remembers !
　How like quivering flames they start,
15　When I fan the living embers
　On the hearth-stone of my heart !

'Tis for this, thou Silent River !
　That my spirit leans to thee ;
Thou hast been a generous giver,
20　Take this idle song from me.

---

7. **Friends I love.** The Lowell home, Elmwood, is situated farther up the river.

10. **Three friends.** Probably Charles Sumner, Charles Ward, and Charles Eliot Norton.

BLIND BARTIMEUS

BLIND Bartimeus at the gates
Of Jericho in darkness waits ;
He hears the crowd ;—he hears a breath
Say, " It is Christ of Nazareth ! "
And calls, in tones of agony,⠀⠀⠀⠀⠀⠀⠀5
Ἰησοῦ, ἐλέησόν με !

The thronging multitudes increase ;
Blind Bartimeus, hold thy peace !
But still, above the noisy crowd,
The beggar's cry is shrill and loud ;⠀⠀⠀⠀10
Until they say, " He calleth thee ! "
Θάρσει, ἔγειραι φωνεῖ σε

Then saith the Christ, as silent stands
The crowd, " What wilt thou at my hands ? "
And he replies, " O give me light !⠀⠀⠀⠀15
Rabbi, restore the blind man's sight.
And Jesus answers, Ὕπαγε.
Ἡ πίστις σου σέσωκέ σε !

Ye that have eyes, yet cannot see,
In darkness and in misery,⠀⠀⠀⠀⠀⠀⠀20
Recall those mighty Voices Three,
Ἰησοῦ, ἐλέησόν με !
Θάρσει ἔγειραι, ὕπαγε !
' Η πίστις σου σέσωκέ σε !

---

1. **Blind Bartimeus.** Mark x. 46.
6. Ἰησοῦ, ἐλέησόν με ! Jesus pity me.
12. Θάρσει, ἔγειραι, φωνεῖ σε ! Be of good comfort, rise, he calleth thee.
18. Ὕπαγε· Ἡ πίστις σου σέσωκέ σε ! Go thy way ; thy faith hath made thee whole.

MAIDENHOOD

MAIDEN ! with the meek, brown eyes,
In whose orbs a shadow lies
Like the dusk in evening skies !

Thou whose locks outshine the sun,
5   Golden tresses, wreathed in one,
As the braided streamlets run !

Standing, with reluctant feet,
Where the brook and river meet,
Womanhood and childhood fleet !

10   Gazing, with a timid glance,
On the brooklet's swift advance,
On the river's broad expanse !

Deep and still, that gliding stream
Beautiful to thee must seem,
15   As the river of a dream.

Then why pause with indecision,
When bright angels in thy vision
Beckon thee to fields Elysian ?

Seest thou shadows sailing by,
20   As the dove, with startled eye, ·
Sees the falcon's shadow fly ?

Hearest thou voices on the shore,
That our ears perceive no more,
Deafened by the cataract's roar ?

---

18. **Fields Elysian.** In Greek mythology, the abode of the blessed
after death.

O, thou child of many prayers !
Life hath quicksands,—Life hath snares !
Care and age come unawares !

Like the swell of some sweet tune,
Morning rises into noon,   5
May glides onward into June.

Childhood is the bough, where slumbered
Birds and blossoms many-numbered ;—
Age, that bough with snows encumbered.

Gather, then, each flower that grows,   10
When the young heart overflows,
To embalm that tent of snows.

Bear a lily in thy hand ;
Gates of brass cannot withstand
One touch of that magic wand.   15

Bear through sorrow, wrong, and ruth,
In thy heart the dew of youth,
On thy lips the smile of truth.

O, that dew, like balm, shall steal
Into wounds, that cannot heal,   20
Even as sleep our eyes doth seal ;

And that smile, like sunshine, dart
Into many a sunless heart,
For a smile of God thou art.

EXCELSIOR

The shades of night were falling fast,
As through an Alpine village passed
A youth, who bore, 'mid snow and ice,
A banner with the strange device
5   Excelsior !

His brow was sad ; his eye beneath,
Flashed like a faulchion from its sheath,
And like a silver clarion rung
The accents of that unknown tongue,
10   Excelsior !

In happy homes he saw the light
Of household fires gleam warm and bright ;
Above, the spectral glaciers shone,
And from his lips escaped a groan,
15   Excelsior !

" Try not the Pass !" the old man said ;
" Dark lowers the tempest overhead,
The roaring torrent is deep and wide ! "
And loud that clarion voice replied,
20   Excelsior !

" O stay," the maiden said, " and rest
Thy weary head upon this breast ! "
A tear stood in his bright blue eye,
But still he answered with a sigh,
25   Excelsior !

---

5. **Excelsior.** This poem was suggested to Longfellow by the arms of
New York State with the motto " Excelsior."

" Beware the pine-tree's withered branch !
Beware the awful avalanche ! "
This was the peasant's last Good-night,
A voice replied, far up the height,
  Excelsior !   5

At break of day, as heavenward
The pious monks of Saint Bernard
Uttered the oft-repeated prayer,
A voice cried through the startled air,
  Excelsior !   10

A traveller, by the faithful hound,
Half-buried in the snow was found,
Still grasping in his hand of ice,
That banner with the strange device
  Excelsior !   15

There in the twilight cold and gray,
Lifeless, but beautiful, he lay,
And from the sky, serene and far,
A voice fell, like a falling star,
  Excelsior !   20

Maynard's German Texts

A Series of German School Texts

CAREFULLY EDITED BY SCHOLARS FAMILIAR WITH
THE NEEDS OF THE CLASS-ROOM

The distinguishing features of the Series are as follows:

The Texts are chosen only from modern German authors, in order to give the pupil specimens of the language as it is now written and spoken. The German prose style of the present differs so largely from that of the classical period of German literature, from which the books in the hands of pupils are generally taken, that the want of such texts must have been felt by every teacher of German.

Each volume contains, either in excerpt or *in extenso*, a piece of German prose which, whilst continuous enough to sustain interest, will not be too long to be finished in the work of a term or two.

The Series is composed of two progressive courses, the Elementary and the Advanced. Some of the volumes of the Elementary Course contain, in addition to the notes, a complete alphabetical vocabulary. In the remaining volumes of the Series difficulties of meaning, to which the ordinary school dictionaries offer no clew, are dealt with in the notes at the end of each book.

In order not to overburden the vocabularies with verbal forms occurring in the text, a list of the commoner strong verbs is added as an appendix to the volumes of the Elementary Course.

The modern German orthography is used throughout.

The same grammatical terminology is used in all the volumes of the Series.

The volumes are attractively bound in cloth, and the type is large and clear.

All the elementary numbers contain a valuable appendix on the strong and weak verbs.

Specimen copies sent by mail on receipt of the price.

No. 1. Ulysses und der Kyklop, from C. F. Becker's *Erzählungen aus der Alten Welt*. An especially easy number. *Elementary.* 21 pages text, 50 pages vocabulary. Cloth, 25 cents.

No. 2. Fritz auf dem Lande, by Hans Arnold. An easy number. *Elementary.* 29 pages text, 28 pages notes, 28 pages vocabulary, 4 pages appendix. Cloth, 25 cents.

No. 3. Bilder aus der Türkei, from Grube's *Geographische Characterbilder*. *Elementary.* 28 pages text, 25 pages notes, 43 pages vocabulary and appendix. Cloth, 25 cents.

No. 4. Weihnachten bei Leberecht Hünchen, by Heinrich Seidel. *Elementary.* 26 pages text, 36 pages notes, 34 pages vocabulary and appendix. Cloth, 25 cents.

No. 5. **Die Wandelnde Glocke,** from *Der Lahrer Hinkende Bote,* by Wilhelm Fischer. *Elementary.* 33 pages text, 24 pages notes, 38 pages vocabulary and appendix. Cloth, 25 cents.

No. 6. **Der Besuch im Carcer,** Humoreske, by Ernst Eckstein. *Elementary.* 31 pages text, 23 pages notes, 30 pages vocabulary and appendix. Cloth, 25 cents.

No. 7. **Episodes from Andreas Hofer,** by Otto Hoffman. *Elementary.* 78 pages text, 18 pages notes. Cloth, 25 cents.

No. 8. **Die Werke der Barmherzigkeit,** by W. H. Riehl. *Elementary.* 60 pages text, 34 pages notes. Cloth, 25 cents.

No. 9. **Harold,** Trauerspiel in fünf Akten, by Ernst von Wildenbruch. *Advanced.* 4 pages introduction, 115 pages text, 18 pages notes. Cloth, 40 cents.

No. 10. **Kolberg,** Historisches Schauspiel in fünf Akten, by Paul Heyse. *Advanced.* 112 pages text, 25 pages notes. Cloth, 40 cents. ·

No. 11. **Robert Blake** (ein Seestück) und **Cromwell,** zwei ausgewählte Aufsätze, by Reinhold Pauli. *Advanced.* 2 pages preface, 93 pages text, 53 pages notes. Cloth, 40 cents.

No. 12. **Das deutsche Ordensland Preussen,** by H. von Treitschke. *Advanced.* With map, 77 pages text, 62 pages notes. Cloth, 40 cents.

No. 13. **Meister Martin Hildebrand,** by W. H. Riehl. *Advanced.* An easy volume. 3 pages introduction, 53 pages text, 35 pages notes. Cloth, 40 cents.

No. 14. **Die Lehrjahre eines Humanisten,** by W. H. Riehl. *Advanced.* 55 pages text, 47 pages notes. Cloth, 40 cents.

No. 15. **Aus dem Jahrhundert des Grossen Krieges,** by Gustav Freytag. *Advanced.* 28 pages introduction, 85 pages text, 41 pages notes. Cloth, 40 cents.

Goethe's Italienische Reise. (*Selected Letters.*) With introduction, 16 pages, map, text, 98 pages, notes, 48 pages. Edited by H. S. BERESFORD-WEBB, *Examiner in German (Prelim.) to the University of Glasgow.* Cloth, 50 cents.

ENGLISH CLASSIC SERIES—CONTINUED.

ADDITIONAL NUMBERS ON NEXT PAGE.

ENGLISH CLASSIC SERIES—CONTINUED.

158-159 Lamb's Essays. (Selections.)
160-161 Burke's Reflections on the French Revolution.
162-163 Macaulay's History of England, Chapter I. *Complete.*
164-165-166 Prescott's Conquest of Mexico. (Condensed.)

New numbers will be added from time to time.

Single numbers, 32 to 96 pages; mailing price, 12 cents per copy. Double numbers, 75 to 158 pages; mailing price, 24 cents per copy.

SPECIAL NUMBERS.

Milton's Paradise Lost. Book I. With portrait and biographical sketch of Milton, and full introductory and explanatory notes. Bound in Boards. *Mailing price, 30 cents.*

Milton's Paradise Lost. Books I. and II. With portrait and biographical sketch of Milton, and full introductory and explanatory notes. Boards. *Mailing price, 40 cents.*

Shakespeare Reader. Extracts from the Plays of Shakespeare, with historical and explanatory notes. By C. H. WYKES. 160 pp., 16mo, cloth. *Mailing price, 35 cents.*

Chaucer's The Canterbury Tales. The Prologue. With portrait and biographical sketch of the author, introductory and explanatory notes, brief history of English language to time of Chaucer, and glossary. Bound in boards. *Mailing price, 35 cents.*

Chaucer's The Squieres Tale. With portrait and biographical sketch of author, glossary, and full explanatory notes. Boards. *Mailing price, 35 cents.*

Chaucer's The Knightes Tale. With portrait and biographical sketch of author, glossary, and full explanatory notes. Boards. *Mailing price, 40 cents.*

Goldsmith's She Stoops to Conquer. With biographical sketch of author, and full explanatory notes. Boards. *Mailing price, 30 cents.*

Homer's Iliad. Books I. and VI. Metrical translation by GEORGE HOWLAND. With introduction and notes. *Mailing price, 25 cents.*

Homer's Odyssey. Books I., V., IX., and X. Metrical translation by GEORGE HOWLAND. With introduction and notes. *Mailing price, 25 cents.*

Horace's The Art of Poetry. Translated in verse by GEORGE HOWLAND. *Mailing price, 25 cents.*

Defoe's Robinson Crusoe. Edited by PETER PARLEY, with introduction and notes. 16₀ pp. 16mo. Linen. *Mailing price, 30 cents.*

The Story of the German Iliad, with Related Stories. With a full glossary and review of the Influence of the Nibelungen Lied through Richard Wagner. By MARY E. BURT. Illustrated. 128 pages, 12mo, cloth. *Mailing price, 50 cents.*

Special Prices to Teachers.

www.ingramcontent.com/pod-product-compliance
Lightning Source LLC
Chambersburg PA
CBHW031248260626
47169CB00007B/2501